SOMETHING HAPPENED IN OUR TOWN

To families who have lost loved ones to racial injustice,
and to those who are working for a future in which diversity is valued
and celebrated — MARIANNE CELANO, MARIETTA COLLINS, & ANN HAZZARD

For protectors, both big and small —JENNIFER ZIVOIN

Published by
MAGINATION PRESS ®
American Psychological Association
750 First Street NE
Washington, DC 20002

Magination Press is a registered trademark of the American Psychological Association. For more information about our books, including a complete catalog, please write to us, call 1-800-374-2721, or visit our website at www.apa.org/pubs/magination.

Book design by Susan K. White
Printed by Lake Book Manufacturing, Inc., Melrose Park, IL

Library of Congress Cataloging-in-Publication Data
Names: Celano, Marianne, author. | Collins, Marietta, author. |
   Hazzard, Ann, author. | Zivoin, Jennifer, illustrator.
Title: Something happened in our town : a child's story about racial injustice /
   by Marianne Celano, PhD, ABPP, Marietta Collins, PhD, and Ann Hazzard, PhD, ABPP ;
   illustrated by Jennifer Zivoin.
Description: Washington, DC : Magination Press, [2018] | "American Psychological
   Association." | Summary: After discussing the police shooting of a local Black man
   with their families, Emma and Josh know how to treat a new student who looks and
   speaks differently than his classmates.
Identifiers: LCCN 2017036137| ISBN 9781433828546 (hardcover) |
   ISBN 1433828545 (hardcover)
Subjects: | CYAC: Racism—Fiction. | Prejudices—Fiction. | Police Shootings—Fiction.
Classification: LCC PZ7.1.C4647 Som 2018 | DDC [E]—dc23 LC record available at
   https://lccn.loc.gov/2017036137

Manufactured in the United States of America
10 9 8 7 6

SOMETHING HAPPENED IN OUR TOWN

A CHILD'S STORY ABOUT RACIAL INJUSTICE

by Marianne Celano, PhD, ABPP, Marietta Collins, PhD, and Ann Hazzard, PhD, ABPP

illustrated by Jennifer Zivoin

MAGINATION PRESS • WASHINGTON, DC
American Psychological Association

Something bad happened in our town.
The news was on the TV, the radio, and the internet.
The grown-ups didn't think the kids knew about it.

But the kids in Ms. Garcia's class heard some older kids
talking about it, and they had questions.

After school, Emma asked her mother: "Why did the police shoot that man?"

"It was a mistake," said her mother. "I feel sad for the man and his family."

"Yes, the police thought he had a gun," said her father.

"It wasn't a mistake," said her sister, Liz.
"The cops shot him because he was Black."

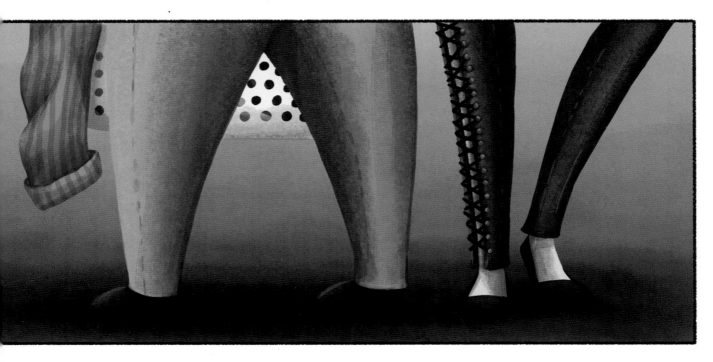

Emma was confused. "He is brown, not black," she said.

"Some Black people have dark brown skin, and some have light brown skin," Emma's father explained.

"'Black' usually means African American. Most of their ancestors were brought here from Africa as slaves."

"I know what a slave is," said Emma. "That's when you have to do whatever the other person says."

"Yes. Slaves had to do whatever White people told them to do. Even after slavery ended, White people didn't let Black people live where they wanted, go to school with White people, or vote."

"Who are White people?"

"White people came here from places in Europe, or Russia or other countries. We are White, even though our skin is light tan."

"Did our family do those bad things a long time ago?" asked Emma.

"Yes," answered her mother. "Back then many White people thought that they were better than Black people, even though it wasn't true."

Liz added: "Some White people still think most Black men and boys are dangerous, even though they're not."

"Was the man that got shot dangerous?" asked Emma.

"No," her mother said. "Shooting him was a mistake. It was a mistake that is part of a pattern."

"Like the pattern on my blanket?" Emma asked.

"Yes. But this pattern is being nice to White people and mean to Black people. It's an unfair pattern."

"Suppose you had a birthday party and invited everyone in your class except the Black kids," her mother said. "How would the Black kids feel?"

"They would be sad," Emma said. "Or mad."

"And YOU would be missing out, because you never know who is going to be your best friend," said Liz.

"And you can help others to be fair," said her mother.

"Like telling Anna to stop teasing Ling about her name?" asked Emma.

Her mother gave her a hug. "Yes, just like that."

In another house, Josh asked his mother:
"Can police go to jail?"

"Yes," said his mother. "Why do you ask?"

"That White policeman who shot the
Black man," said Josh. "Will he go to jail?"

"What he did was wrong,"
said his mother.

"But he won't go to jail," said his father.

"Why not?" asked Josh.

"Cops stick up for each other," said Josh's brother, Malcolm. "And they don't like Black men."

Josh was confused. "Why not? Some police are Black."

"You're right," said his mother. "Uncle James is a police officer, and so is my friend Kenya."

"There are many cops, Black and White, who make good choices," said his father. "But we can't always count on them to do what's right."

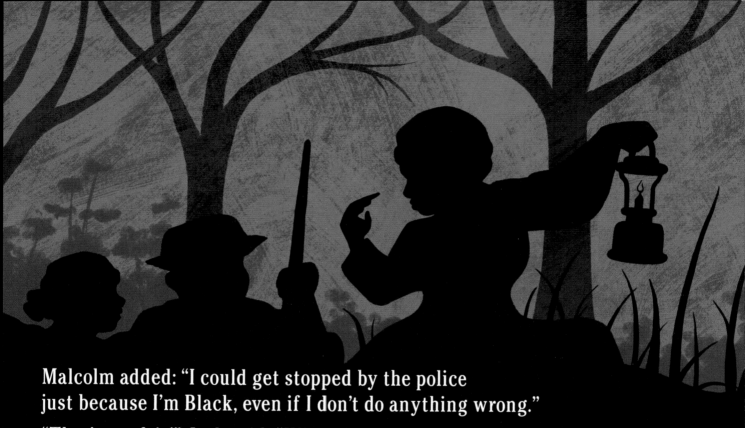

Malcolm added: "I could get stopped by the police just because I'm Black, even if I don't do anything wrong."

"That's not fair!" Josh said. "What if it was a White man in the car? Would the police have shot him?"

"They probably wouldn't have even stopped the car," said his father.

"Sometimes White people are treated better than Black people," said his mother. "But it's not right. Everybody should be treated fairly."

Josh's mother gave him a hug.

"We're proud of who we are. Harriet Tubman, Martin Luther King, Jr., and Nelson Mandela were strong and brave Black leaders. They showed us that we can stand up for our rights and set good examples for others. They were treated unfairly, but helped others learn to be more fair."

"Some people haven't learned yet," said his father angrily.

"Why are you mad?" asked Josh.

"I'm mad that we're still treated poorly sometimes, but I can use my anger to make things better," said his father. "Black people have a lot of power if we work together to make changes."

"I have power," Josh said. "And I'm smart."

His father smiled. "You're right!"

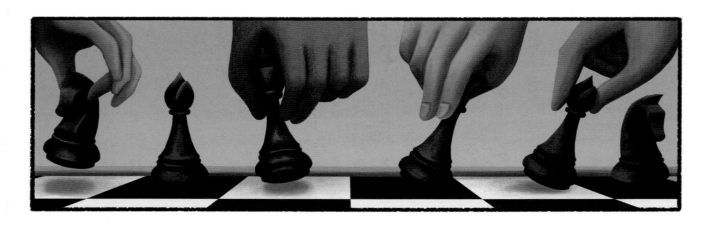

His mother added: "And you can change people's hearts by sticking up for someone who is not treated fairly."

"Like how Malcolm sticks up for me when the kids tease me about my glasses?" Josh asked. "He tells them to step off!"

"Just like that," his parents said.

The next day, a new kid joined Emma and Josh's class.
His name was Omad and he was from a country far away.

Omad didn't know where to sit or what to do because it was
his first day in school. He talked a little bit, but it was hard to
understand him. He said he was learning English.

After lunch the class went outside to play soccer.

Daniel and Sofia picked kids to be on their teams.

All of the kids were picked to be on a team except Omad.

Daniel said Omad probably didn't know how to play because he was new. Sofia said Omad might not be good at soccer.

Josh remembered what his mother said about sticking up for people who are treated unfairly.

Emma remembered what her mother said about unfair patterns and birthday parties.

All of a sudden Omad wasn't alone.
Emma and Josh were leading him to their team.

"We have enough kids on our team," Daniel said.
"We don't need him."

But Josh was ready. "Step off," he said. "He's playing."

"Yeah," said Emma. "We don't want to miss out."

And just like that, Emma and Josh gained a new friend,
and started a better pattern in their school.

NOTE TO PARENTS AND CAREGIVERS

Something Happened in Our Town is designed to be read to children ages 4 to 8, and focuses on bias (prejudiced attitudes) and injustice (discriminatory actions) against African Americans. Before reading this book to children, you may find it helpful to review the material in this Note. In addition to providing general guidance about countering racism with children, this Note offers child-friendly vocabulary definitions, conversation guides, and a link to additional online resources for parents and teachers. This information can help you feel more prepared to address the topic of racial injustice with young children.

While this book focuses on racial bias and injustice against African Americans, the concepts are relevant for all children, including children from other ethnic minority groups and children with multi-racial identities. This book provides messages of empowerment and positive community support, which help children to maintain a sense of balance and safety in our imperfect world. The book's messages of acceptance can also be applied to other differences between people that children may encounter. In addition to bias based on race, children may confront stereotypes based on gender, disability, economic class, culture, family type, or other factors.

COUNTERING RACISM AND RACIAL INJUSTICE WITH CHILDREN

It is understandable that adults want to protect children from life's harsher realities to help them feel safe. Therefore, many parents or teachers may not have discussed racial bias or police shootings with young children. Parents of children from ethnic minority groups typically do talk to their children about racial injustice to prepare and protect them, but may not be sure when or how to start these conversations. For all adults, it is hard to find the right words when discussing this challenging topic.

There are many benefits of beginning to discuss racial bias and injustice with young children of all races and ethnicities:

- Research has shown that children even as young as three years of age notice and comment on differences in skin color.
- Humans of all ages tend to ascribe positive qualities to the group that they belong to and negative qualities to other groups.
- Despite some parents' attempts to protect their children from frightening media content, children often become aware of incidents of community violence, including police shootings.
- Parents who don't proactively talk about racial issues with their children are inadvertently teaching their children that race is a taboo topic. Parents who want to raise children to accept individuals from diverse cultures need to counter negative attitudes that their children develop from exposure to the negative racial stereotypes that persist in our society.

HOW TO ADDRESS RACIAL BIAS WITH CHILDREN

Hopefully, this book will help you begin one of *many* conversations about race and bias that will occur naturally as your child tries to make sense of the interpersonal world. The following are some guidelines for addressing racial bias in discussions with your child and other aspects of your daily life.

General Guidelines
- Take the time to address your child's questions or comments. Do not ignore or sidestep them with blanket reassurances (e.g., "We are all the same inside").
- If your child makes a negative racial comment, ask him or her in a nonjudgmental tone, "what makes you say that?" Your child's answer may provide an opportunity to counter generalizations or to increase empathy.
- Encourage multidimensional views of others. Preschoolers tend to view people as all good or all bad. You can help your child to recognize human complexity and learn to consider both similarities and differences between people in appearance, feelings, preferences, and behaviors.
- Balance your acknowledgement of the reality of racism with messages about hope for change and the availability of help.
- Be prepared to talk about what your child sees and hears. He or she may need help in understanding community events or news stories. It may be difficult to limit your child's exposure to graphic images or overly detailed information about community violence, but try to do so to avoid inducing undue anxiety.

Actions Speak Louder Than Words
Parents can also demonstrate behaviors that promote children's positive attitudes towards racial and cultural diversity.

- Make a proactive effort to regularly engage in activities with individuals from many cultures. Ensure diversity in the media, toys, books, and art that are part of your child's life at home and school.
- Make a rule that it's not acceptable to tease or reject someone based on identity. If teasing occurs, try to find out what underlies the behavior. If the conflict is really about another issue, help your child recognize and resolve that issue. If the underlying reason is discomfort with differences, plan activities to try to overcome that discomfort.
- Demonstrate and encourage acts of kindness toward others and activities to challenge injustice (e.g. protest marches or vigils).

Unique Issues for African American Families
Parents of African American children often face unique challenges in addressing racial bias with their children. Unfortunately, children of color are likely to experience racist encounters. Here are some strategies to keep in mind:
- Strive to promote a positive racial identity in your child by having ongoing conversations and reading books about contributions of African Americans to science and culture, and by participating in community and family activities that contribute to a positive sense of self embedded within an African American community.
- Prepare your child for racist encounters, beginning in preschool. If children feel safe, they can express their disagreement in an assertive but non-aggressive manner with peers who have made racist comments.

- Encourage your child to inform you or trusted adults (e.g. teachers) about racist behaviors from others. Your child's disclosures will give you an opportunity to discuss how to maintain positive self-esteem and respond appropriately to these challenging situations.

VOCABULARY WORDS AND CHILD-FRIENDLY DEFINITIONS

The following are some terms that might come up when you are discussing racial bias and injustice with your child, with child-friendly definitions.

Discrimination: Prejudice is about how you think and discrimination is about how you act. Discrimination is the unfair treatment of a person or group of people because they are different from you. People discriminate against others because of their race, whether they are male or female, the country they come from, their religion, or other differences. Prejudice (bad thoughts about others based on differences) can cause you to discriminate against (treat unfairly) people who are different.

Fairness: Being fair means treating each person in a way that fits what that person needs. For example, it is not fair to give only one child in a family or classroom a treat or privilege for no good reason. It is also not fair to punish one child for no good reason. Being fair doesn't always mean treating everyone exactly the same. Parents don't treat each of their children exactly the same because their children may be different ages and need different things. For example, younger children need more sleep, so they go to bed earlier than older children.

Immigrant: An immigrant is someone who was not born in this country but moved here to make this country his or her home. People who move or immigrate here may not speak our language and may act differently than people who were born in our country do. They may have different ways of doing things based on the way they did things in their country. These differences may cause people to be prejudiced towards immigrants or to discriminate against them.

Prejudice: Prejudice means believing negative or bad things about someone who is different from you without proof. You might have learned or been taught these beliefs. A person could have a prejudiced belief related to skin color, whether a person is a boy or girl, has a different religion, or comes from a different country. For example, a prejudiced belief implied in the story is that because Omad, an immigrant, doesn't speak English well, he will not be good at soccer. Prejudice is a problem because you have already made up your mind or have a bad belief about someone before you know the person, and this is wrong.

Race: Often when people talk about the race of a person, they are noticing the skin color of a person. Black people or African Americans often have skin that is a darker brown than that of White Americans. Most Black people have ancestors that came from Africa. But there is a lot of variety in skin color, even when people belong to the same race. Also, some people have parents who are different races. In America, people have paid a lot of attention to skin color and have used the idea of different races to give some groups of people better treatment than other groups.

Racism or racial injustice: Treating people unfairly (or discriminating against people) based on their race is called racism or racial injustice. Racism starts with a belief that certain races of people are better than others. Racial injustice occurs when people of one race are given more privileges than people who are not of that race.

Slavery: Many years ago, light-skinned people from America and Europe went to Africa. They forced the dark-skinned African people who lived there to come to America, even though the African people wanted to remain in their own land. The Americans treated the Africans very badly during the journey and after they arrived in America. Laws were passed that said that the Americans could own the Africans and the Africans were called slaves. The Americans would not allow the African slaves to make any decisions for themselves. They forced slaves to work for them without paying them. They told the Africans where to live and did not allow them to go to school. They could even sell them as slaves to another American, so that sometimes African parents or children would have to leave their families. Many years later, some White Americans realized the system of slavery that they had developed was very wrong. It took many years and a lot of struggle, but Black people and White people worked together to change the law so that slavery was not allowed anymore. Slavery is no longer legal in our country. However, after slavery ended, for many years there were different laws for Black Americans than there were for White Americans. For example, African Americans had to go to different schools, sit at the back of the bus, and were not allowed to vote. Now, the laws are the same for all Americans, but unfortunately, African Americans are still treated unfairly sometimes.

Stereotype: A stereotype is an idea about a group of people, which could be based on their skin color. You could also have a stereotype based on whether a person is a boy or girl, a person's religion, or other qualities. A stereotype may be true about *some* people in the group. But a stereotype becomes a problem if you have an *extreme* idea that you wrongly think applies to *everyone* in a group. For example, it is true that some Black people are poor and don't have much money. But it would be a stereotype to think that all or almost all Black people are poor. Many Black people have good jobs and have enough money. Here's another example: It might be true that most men are stronger than most women in lifting weights. But it would be a stereotype to think that men and boys are stronger than women and girls in everything. There are lots of ways that boys and girls are both strong. Also, some girls are stronger than some boys in certain situations.

SAMPLE PARENT-CHILD QUESTIONS AND ANSWERS

Something Happened in Our Town includes two family discussions about a police shooting of a Black man. It is likely that the story may prompt discussion in your family of race-related issues. Some discussions with your child may occur as a result of questions he or she asks. And yes, "kids do say the darndest things." It's okay to say, "I don't know. Let me think about it" if you need some time to formulate a response.

This section includes sample responses to possible questions or statements from your child, as well as some conversation-starting ideas for parents. Try not to lecture, but ask follow-up questions and offer ideas as a way to start talking about these issues.

Many discussions can appropriately lead your child to the conclusion that "People may be different on the outside but have many similarities on the inside." However, keep in mind that blanket statements such as "We are all the same inside" may shut down conversation and ignore the reality that there are some general differences in the experiences and perspectives of Black and White individuals in our society due in part to a history of racial injustice.

"Shana's skin is brown and dirty. Why doesn't she take a bath?"
(NOTE: preschool children are concrete thinkers and may confuse dark skin with dirt.) Her skin is not dirty. It is just a different color than yours. People have all sorts of skin colors, just like they have all sorts of hair colors.

"Why do Black boys always act out in class?" What makes you say that?
(NOTE: when a child expresses a negative racial stereotype, it is important to ask "What makes you say that?" Often the answer will provide an opportunity to counter unfair generalizations.)
"Lamar got in trouble twice yesterday." Twice isn't the same as always. Are there some White boys who don't follow rules sometimes? It's not fair to think that all Black boys behave badly just because Lamar made several bad choices. It is not fair to think that all people with a certain skin color are going to act a certain way.

All of us make some good and some bad choices.

"I don't want to play with Jada because she is Black."
(NOTE: If your child expresses a prejudiced belief, stress that those beliefs are not acceptable. You might question your child to try to determine if he or she is frustrated with someone for reasons other than skin color. In that case, you can help your child solve that problem adaptively. Another alternative is to highlight that people have many different characteristics beyond the color of their skin.)
In our family we don't reject people based on their skin color. We choose friends based on what we like or don't like about how they act. Can you think of some ways that you and Jada are alike? What about the games you like to play, the foods you like, and what you think is funny? How do each of you feel when you succeed at something? How do each of you feel when you are left out by other children? Is it possible you are frustrated with Jada for reasons other than the fact that she is Black?

Your child tells a racist joke.
I know you are telling jokes to figure out what's funny and what's not. But it's not a good choice to tell jokes that make fun of someone who is different than you. You have red hair, so how would you feel if someone told a joke that all people with red hair are silly clowns? That's what it's like to tell a joke that makes fun of people's skin color. Did you tell this joke to other kids? It would be a good idea to apologize for telling a mean joke.

"Why do Jamal's parents have different skin colors from each other? You and Dad look the same."
(NOTE: Your child asks about a biracial family.)
Jamal's mother's ancestors came from Africa many years ago, so she is an African American with darker skin. His father is White and his ancestors came from Europe or Russia or some other place. Most people in our country came from somewhere else—people in our family did too. Jamal's skin color is a blend of his parents' skin colors. We are all blended from people from different places. I think that's pretty cool and interesting. But I understand why you might have been confused, since the people in our family have very similar skin color.

"Why did that man shoot those police officers?"
(NOTE: This book focuses on the aftermath of a police officer shooting a Black man in the community. Children may also hear about police officers being shot. The reasons that police officers are shot vary and may not be known in some instances.)
We are still trying to understand why. He might have been a criminal who was trying to keep the police from arresting him and putting him in jail. He might have been angry because he believed police were treating Black people unfairly. Or he might have a brain problem that made him confused about what was really happening so that he felt like he was in danger or on a mission. This is called a psychological problem. However, most people with psychological problems are not violent, just confused and scared. Shooting police is never right, no matter how confused you feel or how unfairly someone acted towards you.

You can prompt other discussions with your own questions. Here are some examples of questions that can facilitate helpful discussions related to diversity and racial justice:

- *"What do you think the world would be like if everyone was exactly the same?"* A box of multicolored crayons can be a helpful analogy for the benefits of diversity.
- *"Do kids in your class ever get teased about being different in some way?"*
- *"How do you think you would feel if you were Black and read this book (or watched this TV show, or saw this movie)?"* This is a good question to ask when you confront stereotypes in media materials.
- *"What is the same about you and (this story character)? What is different?"*
- *"Who are the people in your life who help to keep you safe?"*

SAMPLE DIALOGUES OF SPECIAL RELEVANCE FOR AFRICAN AMERICAN FAMILIES

The following are some questions that African American children, in particular, might have, and some sample responses in child-friendly language.

"Why do White people hate us?"
When we are treated unfairly by White people because we are Black, it feels really bad and can make us believe that all White people hate us. This is surely not the case! Some White people may dislike Black people and treat them badly based on their race. This type of bad treatment may stem from slavery when White people were allowed to own Black people, and laws allowed Black people to be mistreated. Treating Black people badly may have become a habit that is hard for some White

people to break. This is a habit that may have been taught to some White people by their parents and grandparents. There are other White people who do not act like they hate Black people. These White people believe that all races should be treated fairly, which is a good habit. These White people may have been taught this good habit by their parents and grandparents. Treating all races fairly and being open to differences is a good habit for our family to have and share with others.

"Sometimes I wish that I was White."
Other Black people have felt like this, so you are not alone. Perhaps you feel this way because the discrimination and prejudice against Black people makes you feel it would be easier to live here if you were White. This is understandable, but if you were White, you wouldn't be *you*. All of the things that you and I love about *you* would be different if you were not *you*. While it's hard at times to be Black, it's also great to be a part of such a *wonderful* race of people. Some White people want to be more like us because they like our dark skin and even try to tan to darken their skin. They like many things about our culture, such as our music, our dance, our art, our hair, and our skin color! They like our family life, how smart we are, and our determination to be a part of this country even though it's hard when some people treat you unfairly or call you racist names. What's important is accepting and loving ourselves while learning to understand and accept the differences between ourselves and other races. These differences really make the world a great place.

"A White boy in my class called me a (racial slur). If he says that again, I'm going to beat him up."
I can see that you are pretty upset about this, which is certainly understandable! Calling people bad names is never good, and is especially hurtful if the name says mean things about you and your race. But, punching or beating him up is not a good solution. It may even convince the boy and others who are watching that the boy was right to call you the name, because fighting will show you behaving in an out-of-control way. Although it would be quite hard, a better solution would be to calmly state that you don't like being called that name, that it offends you, and that it does not describe who you are. You show the person that you are very strong when you stay calm and stand up for yourself this way. Think of yourself as a superhero surrounded by a force field that makes racist remarks bounce off of you because you have the power of loving and standing up for yourself. If you feel that you cannot remain calm or if it is too hard for you to say these things, ignore the person and walk away. Then it is helpful to talk about what happened with an adult you trust, just like you are doing now.

"Why is Keisha's skin so much lighter than mine? She says she is prettier."
Within the Black community, there are many different shades of skin color, from the darkest of dark to the lightest of light. Some Black people think that lighter skin is better than darker skin and some Black people like darker skin tones more than lighter skin tones. Neither is better than the other. Judging a person based on whether they have light skin or dark skin is wrong. The type of person they are on

the inside is what is most important. Does this person treat others fairly? Would this person be a good friend to me because I know that I can trust and depend on him or her? Is this person honest? These questions are more important than making a decision about a person based on whether they are light skinned or dark skinned.

"What should I do if a police officer stops me?"
(NOTE: Two excellent videos about this topic are "How to Raise A Black Son in America" (TED Talk by Clint Smith) and "How to Deal with The Police/Parents Explain" (YouTube video). Links to these videos as well as other resources are available in the "Additional Resources" found online at www.apa.org/pubs/magination/441B228.aspx.)
As you become older, there may be times when a police officer stops you. *Being stopped by the police is not a reason to panic or run.* It is a time to stop what you are doing, to listen carefully to what the policeman or woman is saying, and then to do what he or she says to do. Speak to the police in a respectful way and be truthful when you answer their questions. It would be okay to say you are nervous and to ask if you can call your parents. If the police stop you, it is important to keep your hands where the police can see them and to not move about quickly. Tell the police if you are planning to look for something in your pocket, on the floor, or on the ground. If the police officer is not treating you fairly, we will figure out how to make things right in the future, but it is safer for you to stay calm and obey the police at that moment.

"Could I get shot by the police?"
Because you are a child and not an adult, there probably won't be situations where you are alone and the police would stop you or show you their gun. If you are with an adult whom you trust and the police stop the adult, listen carefully and follow the instructions from the adult. Also, remember that most police officers never fire their guns during their whole careers because they try to solve problems without violence. There are many police officers who work hard and want to help people.

ADDITIONAL RESOURCES
If you would like further information about related resources, please visit this book's page at www.apa.org/pubs/magination/441B228.aspx. The "Additional Resources" list includes the following:
- Lists of books for young children about: (1) resisting racial bias and advocating for civil rights, and (2) accepting oneself and valuing diversity
- Additional resource lists including books supporting racial pride for children of diverse ethnicities, resources for multicultural families, anti-bullying books, resources about community violence, and resources about racial injustice for older children
- Additional resources for parents
- Additional resources for teachers

Something Happened in Our Town is designed to engage young children in a compelling story as well as spark important discussions about racial injustice. These discussions can help children begin to identify and counter racial injustice in their daily lives. Our hope is that your children, like Josh and Emma, will actively work towards creating a "better pattern" in their community.

About the Authors

MARIANNE CELANO, PhD, ABPP, MARIETTA COLLINS, PhD, and ANN HAZZARD, PhD, ABPP worked together for over two decades as Emory University School of Medicine faculty members serving children and families in Atlanta. All three psychologists have been involved in community advocacy efforts focused on children's behavioral health and social justice. Dr. Celano and Dr. Hazzard have developed and utilized therapeutic stories in individual and group therapy with children and teens. All three authors valued story-time with their children, who taught them important lessons about what children need from adults. This is their first picture book for children.

About the Illustrator

JENNIFER ZIVOIN has always loved art and storytelling, so becoming an illustrator was a natural career path. She has been trained in media ranging from figure drawing to virtual reality, and earned her bachelor of arts degree with highest distinction from the honors division of Indiana University. During her professional career, Jennifer worked as a graphic designer and then as a creative director before finding her artistic niche illustrating children's books. When she is not creating art in her studio, her favorite hobbies include drinking cocoa while reading a good book, swimming on hot summer days, and spending time outside with her family. Jennifer lives in Indiana with her husband and two daughters.

About Magination Press

MAGINATION PRESS is an imprint of the American Psychological Association, the largest scientific and professional organization representing psychologists in the United States and the largest association of psychologists worldwide.